"*everything faces all ways at once* is a gripping, powerfully cathartic, near-perfect work of art."
- God

the san francisco state university chapbook series annually publishes the fiction or poetry of students whose work shows exceptional accomplishment and promise. the 2010 michael rubin fiction chapbook was selected through an open competition by an independent judge. funding for the sfsu chapbook series is provided by the students of sfsu through the instructionally related activities fund. the competition judge for 2010 was terese svoboda.

this is a work of fiction. all of it is true.

grateful acknowledgment is made to the following publications for publishing the works listed: 580 split, "what they don't tell you about bandits"; the chaffey review, "going on ten years"; we still like, "san francisco's been chucking rocks at me from the other side of the moon."

the following stories derive their titles from paintings by rene magritte: "eternal evidence," "the month of the vintage," and "the tomb of the wrestlers."

fourteen hills press, department of creative writing, san francisco state university, 1600 holloway avenue, san francisco ca 94132
www.14hills.net

cover and book design by amber cady
printed by mcnaughton & gunn

summerfield, zulema renee
everything faces all ways at once/ zulema renee summerfield
isbn: 978-1-889292-24-3

everything faces all ways at once

fictions and dreams by zulema renee summerfield

Winner of the 2010
Michael Rubin Book Award

Fourteen Hills Press, San Francisco

"between you and i lies the whole of the universe
and nothing at all."
- extradarklightmagic

"...and the world cracked down the middle."
-marisa crawford,
the haunted house

fictions

what they don't tell you about bandits

bandits have ransacked our tiny seaside village. (and by "tiny seaside village," of course i mean san francisco.) bandits have ransacked our tiny seaside village! they wear fur-lined helmets and carry machetes up their sleeves. they're armed and dangerous. they smell vaguely of rot and the backs of someone's knees.

bandits (and this is widely known) are well-versed in the arts of pillage and plunder. they know how to shatter bones with just their gaze. they know how to crumple a man, they know how to make him plead. everyone knows the fiending is in their eyes, or better, their veins, and it makes their lips quiver when they speak and their fingers, you know, shake.

but the real thing about bandits, the thing they never tell you, is how vulnerable those wild-eyed bastards can be. as if, tucked deep down inside somewhere, nestled in the stink and the rot, the cravings for sugar, the propensity for sin, somewhere in there is something else, some kind of memory, or sound, or habit of light. how to say this?

for example: you come into the house late one night, and it's completely torn up and in shambles, tiles falling from the ceiling, the hallway carpet burnt to a crisp, the cat's tail all tangled and abused. the lights aren't working because the electricity's been cut, there's a ball of molten lava brewing in the sink. you get the idea.

and then there he is, bandit #271, sitting on the edge of the bathtub. he's having a moment, 271 is: he's got his helmet off, he looks a downright mess, and you can't be sure but it looks like he's been crying. you stand in the doorway with your hands on your hips, your eyebrows furrowed as if to say *what the hell is the problem, bandit? what is it now?* and then he looks up, and there's that thing, that quality of light, and he puts his machete down on the floor, and he puts his arms out, just like this, like a child that needs to be held, and you realize that in another life, or rather at a different moment in this one, bandit #271 could take your head off with just one whack, he could end you without thinking twice, sever you and all connection you have to this bleeding and snarled-up world, but that in this moment, this very one right here, bandit #271 is not out to get you, he's not going to do you any harm. rather: bandit #271 is asking you for a hug.

the problem with hugging bandits is that they just might hug you back.

decidedly unbrilliant

decidedly unbrilliant washed ashore. he was wearing overalls and smoking hashish out of a corncob pipe. "how unoriginal is that," decidedly unbrilliant said. he wrote it on a slip of paper, then on the side of a rock using the burnt-out remains of a piece of driftwood— (mysterious, no? how driftwood burns?)— wrote it again on a bench overlooking the sea, on an overturned trashcan, on the forehead of a bloated beached whale.

some kind of confrontation was inevitable. some kind of confrontation was looming large in the sky.

that's when god showed up. "what the fuck are you doing?" he poked his finger into decidedly unbrilliant's chest. "keep your fucking comments to yourself!"

there was no time to respond, because a clean-up crew had come about the whale. "this yours?" the guy asked, a corncob pipe and all the rest. god nodded, shrugged, shook his head, nodded again.

there's no telling what came next. the only way to clean up a beached whale, to *really* clean up a beached whale, is to blow that shit to smithereens.

eternal evidence

anyone might be blinded by possibility. for me, it is the fear that my arms will fall off and go snaking around the room, the features will disembark from my face, i'll trust my torso to a friend and find it riddled with pinpricks in the morning, smeared with chocolate fingerprints— the shape of it, recognizable, suddenly just gone. i call upon angels to fill the room and grant me sight of other things, but when they come they are drunk and rowdy— demons, really, in disguise. they do like this: they pick my arms up off the floor and swing them round their heads, they kiss my legs until those fall off too, they howl into my vagina to test the acoustics there, they string my fingers on a necklace a million miles long. none of this is new. i can say with all fidelity that this pulling apart has been going on for some time, and that angels, or demons, or those people i call my friends, they're no more interested in my horror show than i am in theirs. they're just collectors like anyone else, even the very best of them, just out to get a decent price.

other mornings

if god and you were lovers, at what phase would you be? maybe you're meeting for the first time, playing frisbee in the park, or blind-dated by mutual friends, and there's that fierce and sudden rush— blood to your cheeks, your nipples gone suddenly hard— and a first kiss like a god-damn resurrection, that's how you put it to your friends. or maybe it's been a few months, taking him home to meet the parents, he's seen you without makeup, seen you scream and cry.

dad, this is god.

i know who god is. you think i don't know? i have a master's in theology, mind you.

and god just standing in the doorway, shuffling his feet, or pushing salad around the plate with his fork.

or maybe it's been a few years now, you're pushing thirty, you can't quit smoking, you keep dreaming about men from another life, men you did and did not know. some mornings, you wake up and god is shuffling around the house, whispering words into the phone that you can't quite hear.

other mornings, today at least, you wake up and somehow there are photos of you spread all over the house— you at five, dangling from a branch in your grandmother's backyard, or nineteen, standing in front of a road sign in weed, california— and a mirror, then, propped awkwardly at the end of the hall, a note almost, a message before he left, as if to say, *what is left of you? what wild and burdened thing have you finally become?*

going on ten years

i wake up most mornings obsessed by some thing— a
trail of ants snaking up a wall behind my father's head,
a crowd of children stooping over a rotting orange, a
cat's lopped-off skull in my grandmother's backyard.
my stepfather falls into a hole in vietnam and has to
stay silent for days. my best friend's brother makes a
shadow puppet with his cock. this morning, ten years
ago now, three kids from next door come over to pet a
bunny in the yard. i don't know their names, but still,
the way i see them moving through the slats in the
fence, them crouched and petting like they've never
seen such a thing before. their father had a bunny once,
the boy tells me in spanish, and the sister looks at him
like murder, like *callate, estupido*, but he ignores her,
and when i ask what happened, where'd the bunny go,
he slams one fist into the other, just like that, over and
over and over again, going on ten years.

the month of the vintage

this is a common nightmare: you awaken, and there are ten thousand more of you waiting outside. they've got expectation written all over your face. they wear the same clothes you wear, have the same look you sometimes have of bewildered consternation, they smell exactly as you would smell if reproduced ten thousand times. the common nightmare is this: that you will awaken suddenly to you and more you, all pressing to get into the room.

i am a victim myself. when i come multiplied, i make demands— *stop smoking! vacuum the living room rug! wear a different pair of pants for chrissakes!* my mes rattle the windows and shake the walls. i am more stubborn than the average nightmare. i am more obnoxious, more pushy, more demanding, more crude. i make more noise in the world than other nightmares: i shut others down and i stand in their way. in waking life, i feign perfection, but in dream world— the only real world, after all— i am a terrible and hateful mass.

god, how i love to wake up from this dream! i love that there is only one of me, and if there are ten thousand they are invisible here, in the light of day. or perhaps (how to say this?): there *are* ten thousand of me, there are always ten thousand of us, but in the day i can turn them on and off like switching a dial. ten thousand of me become interchangeable and i am somehow in control.

but okay. enough of that. quiz time: what's the difference between a nightmare and a love poem? because at some point, you have to acknowledge that whoever loves you knows that interchangeability business is bullshit: awake or asleep, they can see through you like seeing through glass. your yous are all of you and they're always hanging around. imagine having to deal with ten thousand yous? something inside me shrinks at the thought.

but this is what love *is*, and you can't change it: when there are ten thousand of you crowding to get into the room, and your lover does not shun them or turn them away. your lover does not scream or cower as any normal person might. instead, your lover blooms and becomes gracious, moving slowly from you to you to you, even if it takes all day.

hello. and who are you? hello. and who are you? hello. and who are you?

notes on a crisis

i go downtown and the bank opens its eyes like this and says "rob me." the bank wants me to be the pacino to its dog-day afternoon. the bank waves million dollar bills in front of my face, taps the bulletproof plastic and says "this? it ain't all that." the bank shoots poison arrows at its own tellers and wiggles its fingers and goes "comeon!comeon!comeon!comeon!" like that, like it's one word and the punctuation and the way his fingers move are part of that word, like the whole dictionary and the entire world of words would crumble and then explode and then crumble some more if you took the punctuation out, that's how much he wants me to rob him, that's how urgent that little finger gesture is. the teller makes a face and it's a million miles long— a face like *i love you/i hate you/ please don't do me any harm.* i think, i should call my mother. "mom, i'm at the bank and some serious shit is about to go down." i always think of my mother when i am sad or sick or some serious shit is about to go down. she taught me to see with some clarity. she taught me to distinguish what is right from what is possible from what is very very wrong.

san francisco's been chucking rocks at
me from the other side of the moon

san francisco's been chucking rocks at me from the other side of the moon. this is *real* conflict. it's like having animals descend upon you, alighting on your outstretched arms, your face tilted towards the sky... but then they turn on you and tear apart your face, shoot venom into your mouth and claw out your eyes.

san francisco's chucking rocks at me, also shooting guns into the air outside my window, stealing my mail, posting shit about me on myspace. and facebook. the internet breeds conflict between san francisco and i. a trolley car rolls over the vulnerable side of my heart (the tender side, the side that lives in fear, the side that's already swollen and bruised), and the city just stands there, just points and laughs and stares. i think, *maybe it will be better if i move?*, but prices are too high, and really, where else would i go?

so i escape into the forest for a few days, survive on foraged mushrooms and squirrels that i hunt myself with a slingshot my brother gave me. a couple of hours later, a ranger shows up. he's got a telephone whose cord stretches all the way across the forest, to the far horizon where his cabin is. i can see the lights blinking there.

the ranger shakes his head, clucks his tongue. "them mushrooms'll kill ya." he hands me the phone. "s'fer you." he's the kind of man i would have loved in another life— mustache, doesn't talk much, hides things under the bed. but then he walks away.

"hello?"

the city is buzzing on the other end of the

line.

    "you can run but you can't hide…" i think i can hear the sound of knuckles grinding, or at the very least being popped.

    birds are out here somewhere. they're just shadows in these shadowed trees. those birds? there's no getting away from those birds. they're all just waiting for their chance.

    but god! my eyes are so tired. vigilance is costly. vigilance is a million dollars on which i haven't got a hold.

the celestial muscles

last night, the clouds pressed their hands against the lower portion of the sky. i know how that feels. i wanted photos to come alive and bodies to unwind, grandmother to arrive from a spot in the mirror, magpies to come and swoop around the room. of course, none of that happened. i spent a lot of time fiddling with the lights and trying to read. it seems of late there is a hollow in my chest where little men go. they come into my dreams and look into my eyes and shrug when i am self-conscious about my hair. they play songs on tiny radios, my men, and can be heard clomping and dance-stepping around the corners of the room, and if you consider the simple fact that the room is my heart, then you will know why i insist, night after night, that you keep your head there (ear pressed to my chest). i have a feeling— of course, this is unfounded— that they perform for me just as i perform for them. and what is that thing they say about an actor and her audience? what is it they say when the lights go out and the players all go home?

the woman i've become

the woman i've become is rampaging through the streets. she's a mess, that one, she really is— her teeth all black and rotting out, extra limbs growing from her sides. she's terrorizing this poor city. she already put her foot through the moscone building, and it's being reported now that she defecated somewhere near washington square. it's all over the evening news. it's all over.

this has been happening for quite some time— the woman i've become doing, ultimately, whatever the fuck she wants. i guess that's what this really comes down to, her plowing her giant hands through booths at the farmers' market, pork chops and silk shirts and pieces of sewer piping all stuck between her teeth. you know this, you know the woman i've become, how she eats people by the bus load, derails commuter trains. she's the one, you know the one, who stays on the left side of the escalator even though you're trying to pass. the woman i've become won't take no shit from no one, that's for sure, it's what she chants as she's charging through the streets: *no shit! no shit! i don't take no shit!* by the end of week one, a couple of high school kids have made it their slogan. by the end of week two, some dude with a myspace page who happens to make t-shirts (you know the dude) he's got 15,000 printed already and they're selling like hot cakes. there's a lot of money to be had, if only we were all that smart. there's a real chunk of change in the woman i've become.

the woman i've become has started writing poetry—
god help her. this is one of her poems. this is the best
of all her poems.

the woman i used to be is raking leaves with god in the
yard. she's stoned out of her mind and tends to talk a
lot. (also, she's kind of a slut.) but i have to say, she does
look good, her hair all long and shiny like that. she
looks better than i've ever seen her, better than she'll
ever look again.

the woman i want to be won't return my calls. three
times today already i've called, and nothing. it's quite
possible the woman i want to be is out of town. it's
quite possible she's never coming home.

the woman i've become is fashioning herself a new coat.
it's stitched from all my old pipe dreams, patches of my
thoughts weary and torn, thread made from varicose
veins and the membranes of my heart. the woman
i've become is fashioning herself a new coat, parading
through the halls, speaking in whispers and shadows
and a creepy and redundant and overwrought dream—
wherein: oh, i don't know, maybe there's a family
reunion of sorts, my dad's a werewolf, my mom's out
in the garden eating leaves, my brothers have formed a
jug band and they're singing dylan hits on a makeshift
stage by the pool. of course, yes, i'm there, this is my
dream after all, and maybe i'm making pasta salad from
scratch or polishing the china or something before the

guests arrive, real good, real best-daughter-ever-like, and later i'll regale them all with stories of my travels, *oh she's so funny! she's so wild and adventurous! let's hope she never leaves!* and i'll do a slideshow and then my award-winning tap routine entitled "Tap This!" and they'll all be laughing and clapping and chanting my name, and i'll serve dessert and then help my sister give birth in the guest bedroom downstairs. *what a woman!* my parents will shout. *what a remarkable daughter we have!* and we're all eating tiramisu and ogling the new baby, coochie coochie coo, and it's the best day ever! the best day of our lives! and we're so happy, so perfect and unassailable and god-swimmingly happy, we won't even notice when the baby spits up, or my dad has a heart attack because he eats too much beef and mayonnaise, or that there are maggots spilling out of the garbage, the dog has cancer of the mouth, bees are starting to swarm outside, and of course, the woman i've become is out there in her new coat, nasty and fat and half-dead, running screaming through the yard.

two revolutionaries

two revolutionaries sleep side by side. one refuses to use the internet. the other one is the internet. the first can't stand light, heat, the sound of someone clicking his fingernails together. the second is working out his obsessions. his obsessions are: the way sugar collects at the bottom of a bowl, the letter q, the death of his father near a riverbed.

"if i believed in money, i'd buy you a new coat," one revolutionary says to the other sometime later in the week.

"what's wrong with this one?" the first asks, hands on his lapel.

"it stinks like the bourgeoisie."

two revolutionaries wrestle in the mud. the first has never seen war before. the second one has— all his dreams are full of severed heads rolling down hills, hands coming to life and walking around.

two revolutionaries are seated at a café. one writes a letter to his mother. "dear mother— this may be the last you hear of me. tomorrow we go into the jungle." he licks the letter, stamps it, walks to the mailbox on the corner. he kisses the envelope, thinking, *i don't care if my comrade sees that i love my mother. true revolutionaries love without shame*. he closes the box and looks up at the sky. there are many birds there.

two revolutionaries are seated at a café. one goes to

mail a letter. when he gets back, the other has suffered a fatal wound to the chest. he is slumped at the café table, the pooled blood like polished glass, like a discarded bandanna. his eyes circle up, just one tiny flicker of life left. he looks the other revolutionary in the eye. "you've betrayed the revolution," he manages, just before he dies. the other does not have time to explain, *it was a letter to my mother! tomorrow we go into the jungle! true revolutionaries love without shame!*

one revolutionary takes another's body to be buried in the jungle. *this is the proper way to go,* he thinks. the body is heavy: heavy as lead, heavy as a fallen comrade, heavy as a revolution gone awry. when he gets to the bus station, the porter slowly shakes his head, over and over and over again.

all trips into the jungle are sold out for the next ten thousand years.

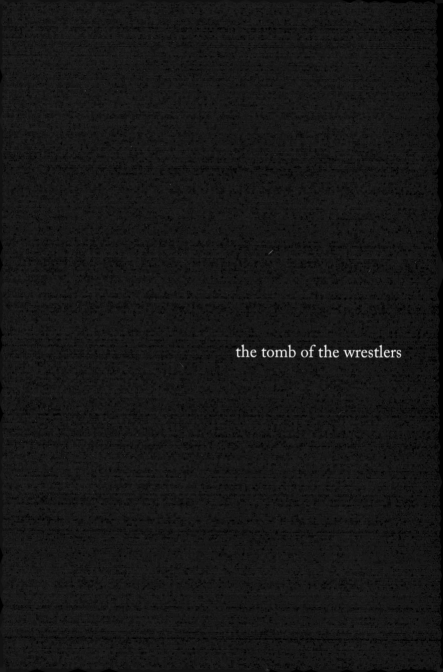

the tomb of the wrestlers

sometimes, the thought is bigger than the room.

dear mother: the thought has become bigger than the room. i am cowering in the corner beneath it, hands clasped, knees bent, chin to knees. the thought is huge and it's taking up the room.

dear mother: a thought has become bigger than the room. i have to tell you that i am falling apart at the seams. every night when i sleep, my shoulders become unstitched from my arms, my legs unravel, buckle, recede. i have four wounds that will not heal, four wounds that have a tendency to pull forth, and just bleed, and bleed, and bleed.

dear mother: remember when you told me to go and meet the neighbors? you said, *i want you to go and meet the neighbors. it's important for you to have a safety net for when anything goes wrong.* i meant to tell you that i did not go and meet the neighbors. i meant to tell you that i did not quit smoking, i don't eat enough, and i drink too much beer. i meant to tell you that i am not well, that when i sleep at night wild animals come into my dreams.

dear mother: i sleep at night and wild elk burst though the sheets. they are massive and hungry and their breath lights up the room. they are starving and wild and their breath lights up the room. i have four wounds on either side of me, and every day i wake up with a small nest of fear inside my chest. those wild animals push against me and ask, *what do you have to be afraid of? what the hell have you got to fear?* and their breath is warm on my shirt, and their breath makes wet on my shirt, and their breath is solid, and their breath will not go. at night i sleep and wild animals stalk into my dreams, cats the size of horses, snakes that swallow my arms, birds and bats that swoop down and take nips at me from the tops of all the trees. *go and meet the neighbors. it's good to meet your neighbors.*

dear mother: i did not go and meet the neighbors. at night, i tangle myself in sheets and dream i've got a thousand lovers, and my hair is long and i wear sassy high heels, i don't smoke, and i am never sad, i have a solid grasp of what goes on in the world, i have a solid grasp of what everything means. i am charitable and kind and easy to trust, i give everything i have and then i give more, i never tell a lie, i never think from greed, i call everyone back who has ever called me, i never think a bad thought, i do not procrastinate, i eat more than just macaroni and cheese.

dear mother: my greatest guilt is that i do not call. i think about that every day, and still i do not call.

dear mother: at night, a herd of wild mothers comes screeching into my dreams. they wave wooden spoons above their heads and demand that i meet the neighbors, quit smoking, stop eating macaroni and cheese. they are something of you and something of other mothers that i have never seen. they are something for me to model myself after.

dear mother: i've been dreaming of something for me to model myself after, but then i wake up and i do the same as always: two coffees and a cigarette, and then find some excuse not to do any more work because i am lazy.

dear mother: i am afraid that i am lazy. i am afraid that a herd of wild animals will come into my dreams and whisk me away and i will not resist because i am lazy, and also, given to being swept away by my dreams.

dear mother: a herd of wild elk and wild men have swept into my dreams. i wear high heels and never make mistakes. my hair is long again and the men buy me drinks in dark bars, and they pull on my pigtails and say *my, aren't you cute*, but what they really mean is sexy. cute means sexy when you are this small.

dear mother: i am still and always have been just this small. do you remember when i was born and even then i was small? nothing, really, has changed.

dear mother: nothing has changed. a herd of wild elk has made their way into my room, and god, i was just trying to sleep, and the neighbors you told me to meet but i never did, they come pounding on the door. *what the fuck is all that racket? who's making the wild elk noise?* and if i had done as you said, gone out to meet the neighbors, this wouldn't be a problem. i could say, as anyone might say to their neighbors, jerry or susan or ted or hassan, *a herd of wild elk has risen from my dreams!* and being neighbors, goodly neighbors, they come in right away, they call animal control, they scoop into their arms the most precious of my things. they take me into their homes and cover me with blankets and make me hot chamomile tea. and even after animal control comes and takes the elk away, the neighbors are *still* good to me, they are *still* my friends, they make me casseroles and bring them over every night, they invite me to all their parties, and this is *exactly* what you'd hoped for, the community you'd told me about, the safety net to protect me from my dreams.

dear mother: i never did go and meet the neighbors, so now when wild animals sprout from my ears and take over the room, snorting and bucking and tearing at my things, the worst that could happen is what happens, is the one thing that you feared most, which is that no one believes me, no one is willing to help me out, and everyone thinks i'm insane.

dear mother: that's a lie. i've spent all day making friends with the neighbors. they love me and they find me so very charming indeed. they take me to dinner and when i cry they ask me what is wrong.

dear mother: the neighbors have invited me to dinner in order to find out what is wrong.

a herd of wild elk has moved into my room!

yeah, well, they're beginning to spoil the vibe around here, jerry says.

yeah, and they stink like shit, says hassan. the neighbors have invited me over for dinner, but they failed to mention the truth, which is that this is less of a dinner and more of an intervention, and they just want all the noise to stop, and they don't give a shit about what's sprouting from my dreams.

dear mother: the neighbors are hosting an intervention. nobody gives a shit about what is wrong, they just want it to stop.

dear mother: the neighbors are here and they're pounding on the door because they want it to stop. this is the only thing we have in common— we all just want it to stop.

if you go, go slow

1. this is what happened: i went over the bay bridge. i had a fear of bridges. it rained. i went to a christmas play. i tried not to weep or sleep during the christmas play. i came back over the bridge. several people have died on this bridge. i thought the bridge was haunted. i waited to see their ghosts. i saw the wet and trailing lights, and maybe that was their ghosts.

2. one man who died was in a pear truck. he was driving to deliver some pears. it was three in the morning. something happened. his truck went over the side. in the morning, when the news broke, his family put out a statement: he was a good man. the bridge people said yes, maybe, probably he was a good man, but he was going too fast, not slow. the truck company people, they too said yes, maybe, probably he was a good man, but he was driving impaired. the accident was his fault, not theirs, because he'd been driving impaired.

3. later, i went to a party. someone said "driving impeared." everyone thought that was mostly funny but really mostly not. i said the thing about the man's family, also about the bridge people and the company that owned the truck. a man is dead now, and no one is taking responsibility, so that is why i said the thing about the bridge and the truck.

4. i read the chronicle. the chronicle is a dying paper. the chronicle is the ghost of a paper. but still, the chronicle says that hospitals are chock full of people

who are afraid. they've all been reading about the bridge and now everyone is afraid. there is a word for this kind of fear. the word for this kind of fear, the fear of bridges, is gephyrophobia.

5. it's the new century and every fear has a name. if you think you are the only one with a specific fear, don't worry: you're not. even that fear has a name, the fear of when you think you are the only person who has a particular fear. the name of that fear is irony.

6. irony is a word that means when everyone is afraid of nothing to be afraid about. this is the story of my life. the story of my life is irony, which is also fear.

7. the bridge is haunted but no one wants to believe me. they say, *oh, you're exaggerating*. they say, *oh, it's the twenty-first century and ghosts don't exist anymore*. so then i revise what i mean. conquering your fears means revising what you mean. "okay, the bridge is not haunted. you're right. but the bridge *is* cursed." everyone looks at me with a blank stare. the blank stare goes on for awhile. then, with no warning, the blank stare turns into laughing. what i said about the curse gets turned into a joke, and then it's the best joke ever, better even than driving impeared.

8. a man from hayward was driving impeared. he was a good man. he did not own the truck he drove, but the truck company owned him. now the bridge is haunted

by the curse of irony. if you drive it, go slow, and have no expectations. you can be a good man, a family man, a man of honor and grace, but a curse is still a curse. which is why the bridge people and the truck people are saying all the time to go slow. if you go, go very, very slow.

uprising

here, then, hands without their bodies: severed at the wrists, wandering the streets. hands bony with grief, veined with desire, wedding rings here, painted fingernails there. they move like spiders through the streets, fingers as feet, scuttling nails across the road. a million hands with bodies unattached, a million hands without eyes or legs or ears or mouths. hands that scurry and move, their bloodied stumps broad disks of red. a million hands that walk, converge. a million hands that pass up streets— now jackson, now fillmore, now market— and come to stand to make a crowd. a million hands with a million silences gather at union square. this is the time that we will watch. wait, now, and let us see— if they will wrap their fingers together and hold one another, or turn their palm faces up, up to see the sky.

everything faces all ways at once

everything faces all ways at once. it has only been a few years now since a group of cartographers came here to prove it. they were the kind of fellows, these cartographers were, that defy all expectation. one minute they're sporting monocles and engaging one another in philosophical quandries, the next they're drunk and rowdy and throwing patio furniture off the roof of the hotel downtown. but in this and all things, they sought the essence of truth: *is true truth possible? isn't every attempt to "map things out," by its very nature, biased and therefore flawed and therefore doomed to fail?* life is a barrel and the more you pour in it the more will spill out, so naturally those map boys were driven to drink.

they came to our town and they set up their equipment (this was years ago now), and they proceeded to prove, once and for all, that— in this place at least— everything faces all ways at once. the most successful of these experiments proved to be the most simple: one cartographer moved off several hundred paces, rounded a corner, ducked behind a tree, and covered his eyes with his hands. another cartographer did exactly the same, only in the opposite direction. after ten minutes or so of hiding like this, the one ventured to radio the other:

"milo to philomingus... milo to philomingus... do you copy?"

        "copy."

"are you paced several hundred paces away?"
          "affirmative."
"are you around a corner?"
          "affirmative."
"have you ducked behind a tree?"
          "affirmative."
"have you covered your eyes?"
          "affirmative."
"and can... can you see me?"

a crackling then, a trembling in the throat, like rain
that scratches when it falls from the sky.

"by god, milo! i *can* see you! i really truly can!"

skeptics, of course, would not only point out the
impossibility of the cartographers' findings, but also
that these "findings" proved nothing, really, at all.

but that didn't stop those map men from downing
two bottles of absinthe, storming the lobby of the
hotel, clawing the furniture to shreds, and ripping the
carpet up with their teeth. you think the impossible is
nothing, a no thing, but then there it is staring you in
the face, down the long black barrel of a telescope, and
you can say— anyone can sit there and say— "they
saw nothing, they saw a no thing, and now the lobby
of our hotel is ruined forever," and that may be true, in
part. the decorative glass is indeed shattered, the carpet
yes it's stained and reeking of booze, the fireplace is

missing more than a few bricks and whistling at night
like a toothless old man. but everything faces all ways
at once, particularly the truth, and on the one hand
you've got a couple of mad and drunk cartographers
who have left town and aren't coming back, and on the
other you've got a hotel lobby that is seriously fucked
and will never be the same, but on the third hand,
which is the last hand, which is comprised of every
hand that's ever been or was or will be again, you've
got a point and it's fixed like this in space, but also it's
shifting, and turning, and moving towards you now,
hurtling through space and time and everything in
between, and it's coming right towards you, and you've
got to watch, you must be very very careful, because
any minute now it's going to come through these walls
and enter this room, and pierce right through your
skeptical, unbelieving, tender human heart.

dreams

dream of war

dream: my nonni's house is in afghanistan and it's being rocketed to the ground. going through the rubble to find clothes. thinking, *there will be children who will need these clothes*, but there isn't much time. more rockets are coming and there's never any time.

everywhere are afghani women, single-file, wandering the roads. they've lost their homes and now they wander the roads. they are tiny, each of them less than five feet tall, and they wear tweed skirts like amber used to wear in spain, shawls spread over their shoulders. one has a face like a crushed apple. another looks like meryl streep. another one looks so much like my mother that maybe she is. they are calm and markedly nonviolent, yet full of loss and rage. they show us the places where rockets come out of the ground. "one minute, it is a field of grass and flowers. the next— blink your eyes— there are rockets coming out of the ground."

dream of class, and anatomy, and how
my mother shattered my knees

dream: everybody's playing around, which is just another way of saying they're fucking with us. it gets so bad i end up in a wheelchair. but that's later. now, mom goes, "follow me," and takes us to a hill overlooking the sea.

there are many mansions. fortresses, really, each buffeted by high, let's call them military-looking walls. cut glass, all that. you can't see inside, but man! if you could? or better, if you could *live* inside? everything would be different. everything would be a dense fog of wish and fulfillment. snap your fingers and the world's a loyal dog sniffing at your crotch.

except that's not how it is. those walls are meant to keep the riffraff out, and we're the riffraff— my brother, my mom, me.

but you can tell she'd rather be called by a million different names, from how she keeps walking away. she's wearing a new jacket and she doesn't want to be associated with us. my mother refuses to get too close.

and by "my mother," of course i mean me.

there's one house looks that just like a ship. it was built to be that way. three stories tall and one whole wall made entirely from glass. we stand at the base of the wall and admire the extravagance there. my brother puts his fingers in his mouth, and now mother is nowhere to be found.

here is what they do in this plate-glass mansion: through an elaborate system of pulleys and underground machines, they pump water up out of the cold grey ocean, filter it, heat it up, filter it again, bring it under and through the walls, heat it again, filter it again, and then it isn't brackish ocean water anymore, but instead, it's a jacuzzi. that's what it means to be rich and extravagant: when you bring the world's water up through the walls to transform it, to make it your own.

but to be clear: this is also a manipulation, because it's obvious it never gets used. the lights are all off in a way that says the jacuzzi is never used. but that's the whole point: build a glorious thing and keep it just out of reach. it's like dangling a carrot on a stick, and then beating someone with it, the stick.

"hey! look at this!" my brother's found some bags that have washed up on shore. now his shirt is gone. poor thing. sooner or later it's gonna be his shoes, and then his pants, and then him.

"look! look!" he's shoving his hands inside the bags. it's like christmas without all the booze. "this is just what i want forever!" and the way he says it, you know it's true. the bags are filled with powdered cement hardened by the sea. they've ripped, those bags, in the undertow, and i know just how that feels. i reach into a bag and pull out some cement.

"look, everybody! remember what i was saying about needing solid ground?" i can feel them all around me— colleagues, teachers, uncles, the people i call my friends— and this is the name of vindication. "see, i told you. i told you i'd eventually find it." but when i look again it turns out no one is there.

my brother rips one of the bags open more. it's filled with crabs and clams. "mom said this is what a vagina looks like," he says, poking a stick at a clam.

　　　　　　"mom doesn't know what she's talking about," i say, but then i see that she does. this one clam is as big as a whale, and i put my hands in and crack it open— all blood and tongues of meat squirming around inside. that's exactly what it is when i am on fire: rolling fists of blood and gut that i try but cannot keep inside.

which is another way of saying: in sleep i need sex like it's air. in sleep i'm screaming and slapping at the walls. behind the walls? nothing. behind the nothing? more walls.

that's how i end up in a wheelchair. i am less than perfect so my mother shatters my knees. i'll spare you that part, the gruesomeness of my mother shattering my knees. instead, i'll tell you how the world is different when you must move in a new way. how everything changes when your mother shatters your knees.

dream of strange men

dream: for the first time, i am beginning to understand what duplicity really feels like, though of course i would never give it that name. it's understood in a dusty way, a peripheral way, like fireflies shining above a canopy of tangled and poisonous trees. i show some strange men into a room where other strange men play. i say, "listen up, strange men! all you strange and little men. fuck you. now play with these other strange men." the rug in the room is as thick as the hair on their chests. i think, *i want to be broken in half*, and i'm going to do it, i'm just about to, but then my hands snap off and go running around the room. my hands say all the things my mouth cannot, which is mostly like *fuck you* and mostly like *play nice* and mostly like *leave me alone.*

dream of the old woman

dream: i am and always have been haunted by an old woman. she suffers from a crumbling face. she's behind me every time i turn around. we're walking along and we keep encountering each other on all these hidden streets. we *are* these hidden streets. i go to every house i've ever lived in and this is like stringing beads, like drawing maps. the people who live there live there now and they mostly but mostly do not welcome me with open arms. the whole world is like that, sometimes, like open but also never and not open arms. my ghost with a squashed face and i, we go to a lookout tower at a mostly closed museum. we huddle together in a window and watch thousands of birds swarm and swirl around. my ghost is not impressed. she's seen the whole world like this before— the vistas, the tops of all the trees. views like this are the views from heaven. so then she pulls out some old bread she's been carrying around. it's wrapped in a paper napkin. the security guard comes over. "hey! no eating in the museum," even though she's not eating it. it's still all wrapped up, like a mummy, like a dead thing, like a thing you want to keep alive even as it isn't.

dream of chaos

dream: i'm in my workshop class. there are twice as many people as usual; also, they are twice as young. someone's story is up. that's what we say: their story is up.

peter orner leans back in his chair. he has the up story in his hand. he seldom wears a coat. "you know, this story reminds me of a movie i once made about chaos." the movie comes on. the movie: someone (is it me?) is loading towels into a front-load dryer. the towels tumble for awhile, and then bam! just like that they start to multiply and grow! exponentially! hand towels the size of beach towels burst out of the dryer and scramble across the floor! they take over the hallway, the outside stairs! towels overrunning the streets! they climb buildings and dangle from trees! towels on all the buses! towels punching their fists through the windows of all the buses!

(and so on.)

it's chaos!

did i say this? the film is about chaos.

i look down at my own story. it is not up yet, but it will be soon. i realize then that i have attached, to each copy of my story, a wooden ornament that i made but forgot about making. they are carved wooden hands, posed in the act of writing.

the kid next to me glances over. "oh, you made one of those for each copy of your story? that's cool." he's got a nervous and unnerving laugh. "ha ha! i just ripped open my chest and tore out my own heart for my story." ha!

i'm outside then. my hair is back, it's long again. i'm barefoot and i'm doing this dance that i do in my dreams. you know the one: swing a leg in the air until you helicopter away. i'm just about to helicopter away when i see glass on the ground. there's broken glass all over the ground.

"that's chaos," i think.

there's chaos all over the ground.

dream of monsters

dream: they said, *take your monsters out*, they said, we want to see your monsters, pin your monsters through the shoulder to a wide white wall. your monsters as bone crushers and crushed, glass in the teeth under a fierce dead moon. monsters like being rolled over by a train, like wild unseen boys tumbling through the trees, everything punched with holes, everything fallen apart. your monsters as fallen apart.

the smell of fear, then, how fear travels at the speed of light. the night is a spiked heel in the center of your chest.

so come now: show us what you've got.
please, please, show us what you've got.

dream of uh-oh

dream: someone brings an x-ray machine to work.
turns out i'm pregnant.

dream of rattlesnakes

dream: rattlesnakes! everywhere! there's rattlesnakes everywhere! oh my god! a rattlesnake bit my grandpa on the arm and now he's going to die! everything is snakes! that rug! it's a snake! let's get out of here! go to an art show! holy shit! that's not art! it's rattlesnakes!

dream of gender, oversimplified

dream: the difference between a male bird and a female bird is that male birds come in many colors, and female birds are just brown. you can always tell the difference.

later, i get stung by a scorpion, even though the scorpion is dead. ricky ramos is there.

"you've known me the longest out of everyone here."

it's a party and he's old enough to drink.

dream of ghosts

dream: my new house has been taken over by ghosts. i know this because a.) they lit a stick of incense while i was sleeping (i *never* light a stick of incense while i am sleeping), and b.) they bought a new fan that's big and whirls fast and keeps things fairly cool at night. it's a nice fan, real high-end, does a great job of keeping things cool at night... but *still*. it's like, get out of my house, ghosts.

dream of when they built a mall

dream: in order to stave off budget cuts at school, they build a mall somewhere near the quad. this makes perfect sense— you gotta spend money to make money, i suppose. everyone's got to do their part to keep the mall afloat. peter orner has to work at the frozen yogurt stand. matthew clark davison sells glittery t-shirts at a glittery booth.

it's coming up on my stepdad's birthday, so liz and i go to the white-linen-suits-and-also-camping-gear store. bill loves white linen suits. and also camping gear. everything costs two hundred dollars, or five hundred dollars. that's what all the tags say: "200 dollars" or "500 dollars." i can't afford 200 dollars or 500 dollars. *maybe something in the camping gear*, i think, but i can't afford any of that either. and then liz says "look! they sell orange julius now in plastic bottles shaped like swimmers!" so of course we have to get some of those. my swimmer has a hole in it.

peter orner's other job is to ride a mechanical whooly mammoth around the perimeter of the school. i know this because it's my job to drive a security van around. when i drive past him there's this look between us like, "i know that you know that i know that you're kind of laughing at me because i'm riding a mechanical whooly mammoth around, and that's cool."

and then i'm back at the mall and this little girl has started her period and it's my job to tell her all about how it "works." we're buying maxi pads when her mom shows up. it's awkward. i'm like, "a third grader shouldn't be wearing tampons," and she's all, "why not?" and i know what to say but not how to say it, so then all that awkwardness? it just gets worse.

and then i go to my workshop class and try to tell them all about the dream i just had. ("they built a mall! you had to ride a mechanical bull!") but nobody cares. they're all just trying to get past me out the door. there may have been an explosion somewhere.

when i get home, the cat has peed everywhere. everything is ruined.

dream of when we were the same

dream: terrible? am i terrible? i don't think so. like you,
i'm just another like-you machine.

dream of change we can believe in

dream: there's this great big banquet hall and everybody's there: me, my mom, ricky ramos, barack obama, a whole bunch of senators and big wigs that need to get in good with barack obama, and so on. it's hot as hell and we've just been hiking in the most stunning and beautiful place ever, all waterfalls and birds swooping out of crystalline skies, and i'm wearing this adorable red bathing suit with little white polka dots, only problem is it squishes my boobs something awful, it's like i hardly have any boobs at all, and i really want ricky ramos to look at my boobs, which he does for a little while, i mean for at least one minute or one second, and that feels good, even though it's short-lived. but then he gets distracted by this chart that all the boys have made with barack obama's help. it's a chart that keeps track of how tall you are, or maybe how tall you might get to be if you're lucky. all the boys are gathered around and barack obama is gathered around and i want to gather around too but you can tell it's a thing that is mostly for boys. god, i love ricky ramos.

but it's getting close to show-and-tell time, and i'm thinking all about what it is that i have to show and tell. leslie puts on a three stooges movie that she bought at a thrift store. everybody just loves it because everybody just *loves* leslie. they're all, *where did you get this movie? oh, a thrift store?!* all, *leslie's so great! she got this movie at a thrift store!* and you can tell they're just pretending they want to know the title of the movie and the name of the thrift store, *pretending* they're going to go out as soon as this gig is over and get the same movie at the same thrift store. it's obvious they're not pretending for anyone's sake but their own.

now it's my turn for show-and-tell. i had announced earlier that i was going to show a scene from a movie, a joke from the movie *ghost* starring patrick swayze and whoopie goldberg, but i haven't got the tape wound to where it needs to be and i can't stop giggling because ricky ramos is in the room and all i do around him is stop whatever i'm doing and giggle, and sometimes also hope that he will look, i mean stare, at my boobs. i have about a billion rings on my fingers and they keep sliding around because they are too many and too big. and also i have to go, it's my time to show and tell, and everyone's getting impatient, like, *another movie? leslie just put on a movie!* in a way that means my movie doesn't stand a chance. but i can't seem to do anything except stand around and giggle, and then i realize that the problem is that i don't *want* to stand around and giggle, and i don't *want* to show part of the movie *ghost* starring patrick swayze and whoopie goldberg, and i don't *want* to try to measure my height with barack obama, because all i really *want* to do is to get onstage and read some of my own writing, but i can't because it's not really that kind of show-and-tell, and also, mostly, i'm scared— not of what people will think of my writing, but of what people will think of me.

i don't know what happens with that. i still love ricky ramos, and maybe he loves me too because of the way he might be sitting in his chair. i go into the lobby, and barack obama is in the lobby. now is my one chance in my whole life to say something to barack obama, and that's the sort of thing you can't pass up, because you're an asshole if you pass that up— not an asshole to the world just an asshole to yourself, which is the worst kind of asshole to be, when you think about it.

so i go over and i catch him by the cookie table and i say, "mr. president, i want to tell you something that maybe not a whole lot of people tell you but that i think is important for you to hear: i think you are doing a pretty good job." of course, i don't mean that he's accomplishing everything he set out to accomplish, and of course i don't know the minutia of what he does or even what's going on, and i probably say this, like, "look, sir, i'm kind of ignorant and i don't even know what's really going on," but the point, and i know this is true because i have an angel that lives near my shoulder that told me this was true, is that he's trying as hard as he can, and i don't think a lot of people try as hard as they can, so i just hope that someone every now and then is saying that out loud, maybe hopefully michelle: *you are doing a good job because you are trying as hard as you can.* and also because this is my only and probably last chance to say something to barack obama, and what did my poet friend once say? something about the presence of glory? something about pressing it to stay?

i lean my head against the wall and close

my eyes so i can think straight. i'm always thinking straight but it has to be with my head against the wall— old habits and they're impossible to kill— and you can tell barack obama is interested in hearing what i have to say, but after all he *is* the president and the president simply can't spend too much time with just one person— what would the papers say?— so the room and how it's pulsing, *what is this about?*

the truth is, it's about everything. it's about health care and it's about the environment and it's about offshore drilling and extraordinary rendition, and it's about equal rights for all citizens, everyone we know and love and do not yet know to love, and it's about the water and how it's not safe to drink anymore, and it's about human rights in china and human rights in cuba and human rights in iran, it's about the people streaming into this country and *why* they are streaming into this country, it's about policies and the policies behind those policies and the policies behind those, and it's about campaign finance reform and who's cuddling who and who's sucking whose dick, it's about reality and the puncture points in that reality, it's about thousands and thousands and thousands of soldiers, arms torn off, brains rattling from explosions, maimed and forever different, half-ways or all ways dead.

which is really just another way of saying this: that lately, the whole world is a hand and it's pressing on my heart. i read the paper every morning and i cry at what i read. the whole of life is pressing on my heart. *that* is what i want to say: that i have seen glory, pressing here, pressing there, but in the end, i have no idea how to interpret it. i have no idea what it means.

acknowledgments

for my many families: immediate, extended, step, half, broken and put-together again; far away and right next door; at home and also out tumbling in the world like so many scattered seeds. i love you and i hope you know who you are.

and for my people ringing cowbells: keep on ringing. the world needs your song.

and for my little friends who, as yet, are not tall enough to ride: thank you for bringing so much joy into my life.

and for nona, michelle, peter, matthew, and truong: i hope it's not weird to say this, but i love you. i really really do.

and for leslie and tamara, my earliest and most enthusiastic readers. i carry you in my bones.

and for amber lea cady: what's that smell? it's genius seeping out of your pores.

and lastly, by which i mean firstly, always, for tucker: you are everything. i love you one million and one.

about the author

zulema renee summerfield received her mfa in creative writing from san francisco state univeristy. she is the author of this book and many more to follow. she would like to extend a very warm thank-you to yoko ono for taking the time to blurb this book. *

www.zulemasummerfield.com

*disclaimer: yoko ono has not actually blurbed this book. yet.